JACKIE RABBITSON
CENTER FIELDER

RED KOWASAKI
RELIEF PITCHER

PONY PEREZ
SHORTSTOP

SANDY KOFOX
STARTING PITCHER

HAMMY SOSA
CATCHER

WALTER WOMBAT
DESIGNATED HITTER

LARRY BOA
THIRD BASE

Fuzzy Baseball

To SANTI

PLAY BALL!

SINCE STEVEN GURNEY

John Steven Gurney

PAPERCUTZ™

New York

Fuzzy Baseball

Created by John Steven Gurney

Dawn Guzzo – Design and Production

Jeff Whitman – Production Coordinator

Shannon Eric Denton – Editor

Bethany Bryan – Associate Editor

Jim Salicrup
Editor-in-Chief

ISBN PB: 978-1-62991-477-0
ISBN HC: 978-1-5458-0435-3

Printed in India

Papercutz books may be purchased for business or promotional use.
For information on bulk purchases please contact
Macmillan Corporate and Premium Sales Department at
(800) 221-7945 x5442.

Distributed by Macmillan
2nd printing, March 2019

JOHN STEVEN GURNEY

Fuzzy Baseball

For Molly, Jesse, Kathie,
and three World Champion teams:
The 1980 Philadelphia Phillies,
The 1986 New York Mets,
and The 2004 Boston Red Sox

PONY PEREZ
SHORTSTOP
24

PERCIVALE PENGUINO
RIGHT FIELD
7

KIT OCELOT
PITCHER
45

BO 'THE GRIZ' GRIZZLY
MANAGER & FIRST BASE
34

SANDY KOFOX
PITCHER
32

RED KOWASAKI
PITCHER
29

KAZUKI KOALA
RIGHT FIELD
19

PAM THE LAMB
LEFT FIELD
8

PEPE PERRITO
SHORTSTOP
13

JACKIE RABBITSON
SECOND BASE
42

HAMMY SOSA
CATCHER
21

LARRY BOA
THIRD BASE
10

WALTER WOMBAT
CENTERFIELD
44

THE FERNWOOD VALLEY FUZZIES

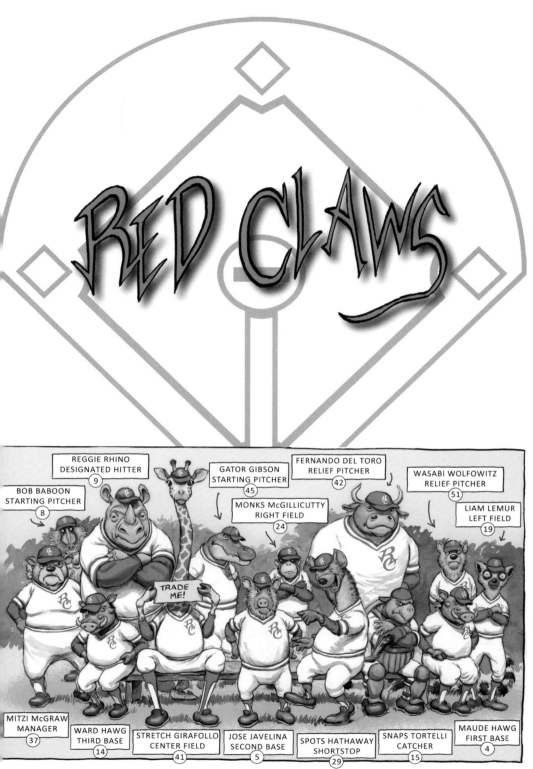

THE ROCKY RIDGE RED CLAWS

INTRODUCING
THE FERNWOOD VALLEY

**THESE
ARE THE
GOOD
GUYS!**

THIS LITTLE
DOG HAS SPEED
AND SMARTS.

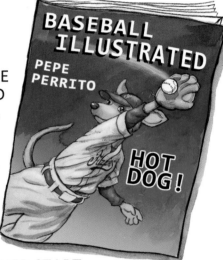

PAM GOT HER START
ON THE FUZZIES'
PETTING FARM TEAM.

JACKIE RABBITSON-
FASTEST FEET IN
THE BIG LEAGUES.

BO "THE GRIZ" GRIZZLY-
ALL STAR SLUGGER
AND MANAGER.

HAMMY SOSA - THE FUZZIES'
CONFIDENT CATCHER

FLIMSTEINS FINE FASHIONS

HAMMY SOSA SAYS

"You don't have to work hard to look this good. Just shop at **FLIMSTEINS**"

THE GRIZ

LARRY BOA
SNAKE
SNACKS

LARRY BOA-
COLD-BLOODED,
BUT
WARM HEARTED

**YET, DESPITE ALL THIS TALENT, THE FUZZIES ALWAYS
LOST TO THE ROCKY RIDGE RED CLAWS.**

INTRODUCING
THE ROCKY RIDGE

*THESE ARE
THE BAD GUYS!*

THE THREE MAIN REASONS
THAT THE FUZZIES
CAN'T SCORE AGAINST
THE RED CLAWS

FIELDING

PITCHING

MONKS McGILLICUTTY

RIGHT FIELD

GATOR GIBSON

PITCHER

FERNANDO DEL TORO

RELIEF PITCHER

MORE PITCHING

WAS THERE ANYONE OUT THERE WHO BELIEVED THAT THE FUZZIES COULD BEAT THE RED CLAWS?

INTRODUCING
BLOSSOM HONEY POSSUM
THE WORLD'S BIGGEST FERNWOOD VALLEY FUZZIES FAN

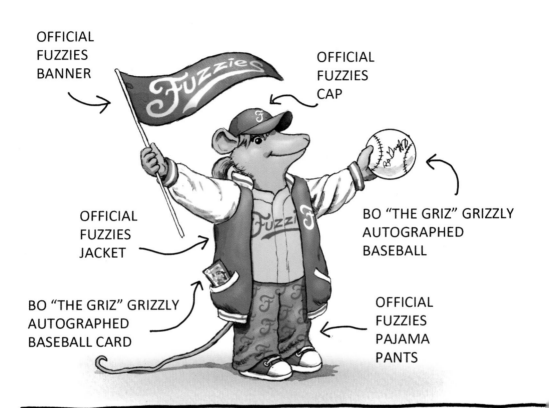

OFFICIAL
FUZZIES
BANNER

OFFICIAL
FUZZIES
CAP

OFFICIAL
FUZZIES
JACKET

BO "THE GRIZ" GRIZZLY
AUTOGRAPHED
BASEBALL

BO "THE GRIZ" GRIZZLY
AUTOGRAPHED
BASEBALL CARD

OFFICIAL
FUZZIES
PAJAMA
PANTS

BLOSSOM WOULD CHEER FOR THE FUZZIES EVERY TIME THEY PLAYED THE RED CLAWS.

THE FUZZIES WILL WIN! THE FUZZIES HAVE HEART! THE FUZZIES HAVE TEAM SPIRIT!

COME ON, GUYS! YOU CAN DO IT!

BLOSSOM NEVER GAVE UP HOPE.

YOU'LL GET 'EM NEXT TIME!

ALMOST NEVER...

YOU GUYS STINK.

THEN, SHE MADE A DECISION.

I'M GOING TO LEARN TO PLAY BASEBALL!

BLOSSOM PRACTICED FIELDING.

SHE PRACTICED BASE RUNNING.

AND SHE PRACTICED BATTING.

SEE THE BALL, HIT THE BALL.

SLIDE!

CRACK

BLOSSOM'S PRACTICE PAID OFF! SHE MADE THE TEAM!

GAME DAY

THE FIRST EIGHT-AND-A-HALF INNINGS DID NOT GO WELL FOR THE FUZZIES.

SANDY KOFOX WAS PITCHING GREAT. HE STRUCK OUT EVERY BATTER EXCEPT REGGIE RHINO.

OH, NO, NOT AGAIN.

UNFORTUNATELY, EVERY TIME REGGIE RHINO WAS UP HE HIT A HOME RUN. AND HE WAS UP THREE TIMES.

EARLY IN THE GAME, THE FUZZIES GOT A FEW HITS, BUT THE RED CLAWS' FIELDING PREVENTED THE FUZZIES FROM SCORING ANY RUNS.

SHORTSTOP SPOTS HATHAWAY MAKING AN AMAZING BEHIND-THE-BACK-STANDING-ON-ONE-FOOT CATCH.

LIAM LEMUR LEAPING IN LEFT FIELD!

MONKS McGILLICUTTY MAKING IT LOOK EASY IN RIGHT FIELD.

AS THE GAME PROGRESSED, GATOR GIBSON'S PITCHING GOT BETTER AND BETTER.

BY THE NINTH INNING HIS PITCHES WERE UNHITTABLE.

THE BOTTOM OF THE NINTH INNING. THE FUZZIES' LAST CHANCE.

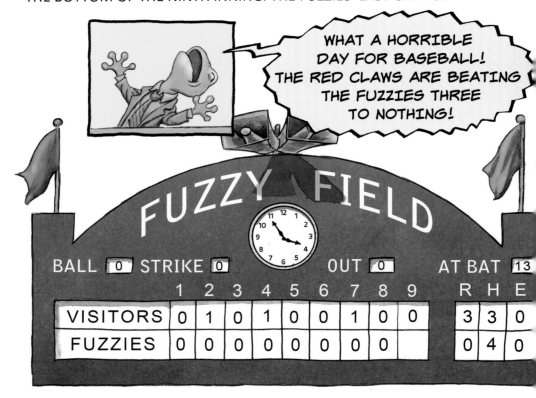

WHAT A HORRIBLE DAY FOR BASEBALL! THE RED CLAWS ARE BEATING THE FUZZIES THREE TO NOTHING!

FUZZY FIELD

BALL 0	STRIKE 0				OUT 0			AT BAT 13

	1	2	3	4	5	6	7	8	9	R	H	E
VISITORS	0	1	0	1	0	0	1	0	0	3	3	0
FUZZIES	0	0	0	0	0	0	0	0		0	4	0

BLOSSOM WAS NOT SURPRISED THAT THE FUZZIES WERE LOSING. BUT SHE WAS SHOCKED AT HOW THEY WERE ACTING. THE FUZZIES DID NOT HAVE TEAM SPIRIT. THEY DID NOT HAVE HEART.

THE RED CLAWS WERE SLAPPING THEIR PAWS AND SMACKING THEIR TAILS. THEY WERE HOOTING AND HOWLING AND GRUNTING AND MAKING FUN OF THE FUZZIES. THEY WERE ACTING LIKE A BUNCH OF... ANIMALS!

THE WORST PART WAS THAT THE FUZZIES WERE ACTING LIKE A BUNCH OF LOSERS.

PEPE KNEW JUST WHERE TO SWING AND...

| ONE OUT, RUNNER ON SECOND... | JACKIE RABBITSON WAS UP NEXT. | GATOR BENT HIS TAIL UP AND PITCHED A FAST BALL. | JACKIE SHIFTED HIS STANCE, SPREAD HIS PAWS OUT ON HIS BAT, AND LAID DOWN A PERFECT BUNT. |

PLINK

RED CLAWS CATCHER "SNAPS" TORTELLI SCRAMBLED TO GET THE BALL AND THREW IT TO FIRST, BUT JACKIE WAS SAFE. AND PEPE RAN TO THIRD.

PEPE RUNS TO THIRD!

GATOR STOMPS AND GROWLS.

SAFE!

JACKIE RUNS TO FIRST!

"SNAPS" TORTELLI THROWS TO FIRST BASE.

LARRY BOA STEPPED UP TO THE PLATE. GATOR CURLED HIS TAIL TO THE LEFT AND PITCHED A CURVE BALL. LARRY DIDN'T SWING BUT...

RED CLAWS MANAGER MITZI McGRAW WALKED OUT TO THE MOUND.

MITZI SIGNALED TO THE BULL PEN. RED CLAWS STAR RELIEF PITCHER, FERNANDO DEL TORO, CHARGED TO THE MOUND.

THE FUZZY'S DUGOUT WAS SUDDENLY SILENT AGAIN.

BLOSSOM COULD NOT STAY QUIET... AND NEITHER COULD ANYBODY ELSE!

FOUR TIMES FERNANDO SNORTED, STOMPED HIS FOOT, WOUND UP, AND THREW A LIGHTNING FAST PITCH.

AND FOUR TIMES THE GRIZ DID NOT SWING. HE DID NOT TWITCH. HE DID NOT EVEN BLINK.

THREE BALLS AND ONE STRIKE. FERNANDO WOUND UP AND THREW A FASTBA
DOWN THE MIDDLE OF THE PLATE. THE GRIZ TOOK A BIG SWING AND...

THERE WAS NO JOY IN FERNWOOD VALLEY.

TWO OUTS, BASES LOADED.

THE NEXT BATTER WAS FUZZY'S CATCHER HAMMY SOSA.

HOLD ON HAMMY, I'M TAKING YOU OUT, AND I'M PUTTING IN BLOSSOM.

THE ROOKIE?

WHAT? SHE'S THE TINIEST ONE ON THE TEAM!

HUH?

EXACTLY! THAT MEANS THAT SHE HAS THE TINIEST STRIKE ZONE ON THE TEAM. FERNANDO PROBABLY WON'T BE ABLE TO THROW STRIKES ON HER. SHE MIGHT BE ABLE TO WALK IN A RUN.

THE END

AND NOW A MESSAGE FROM FERNWOOD VALLEY FUZZIES
ALL-STAR CATCHER HAMMY SOSA.

YOU KNOW, WHEN I'M NOT PLAYING BASEBALL, THERE'S NOTHING THAT I ENJOY MORE THAN SITTING DOWN WITH AN EXCITING GRAPHIC NOVEL! TURN THE PAGE TO SEE A FINE SELECTION FROM THE GOOD FOLKS AT PAPERCUTZ.

Don't Miss Fuzzy Baseball #2 "Ninja Baseball Blast"

WATCH OUT FOR PAPERCUTZ

Welcome to the first, fast- (and foul-) ball-filled FUZZY BASEBALL graphic novel, by the home team's John Steven Gurney, from Papercutz, those denizens of the dugout dedicated to publishing great graphic novels for all ages. I'm Jim Salicrup, Editor-in-Chief and Head Coach.

FUZZY BASEBALL combines America's favorite pastime with two other All-American cultural traditions: comicbooks and funny animals. Like most "funny animals," the characters in FUZZY BASEBALL act far more like humans than actual animals. Papercutz publishes a lot of books filled with comics—called "graphic novels"—that feature animals. We start with the very first animals that ever walked the earth, in DINO-SAURS, a light-hearted, but fact-filled four volume graphic novel series. But the dino-action doesn't stop there! DINOSAUR EXPLORERS sends a group of kids and scientists back in time—even before there were dinosaurs—to trace the origins of these creatures from the Paleozoic to the Cenozoic! And if you want to see a Sci-Fi twist on the future of dinosaurs, check out MANOSAURS—a group of teenage dinosaurs who are half human and half dinosaur.

But we don't only publish graphic novels about extinct creatures. We also publish a lot of graphic novels about cats! So many, that we should probably change our company name from Papercutz to Papercatz! There's PUSSYCAT, a typical housecat with its wacky adventures—written and drawn by Peyo, the world-famous creator of THE SMURFS! CHLOE, the star of her own Charmz series also has a pet cat called Cartoon. He's become so popular that there will soon be the CHLOE'S CAT CARTOON graphic novel. Also coming soon is CAT & CAT, about a girl named Cathy and her cat.

We even published a graphic novel about what seems to be a regular cat, but she actually talks...and is a movie star. You have to get SCARLETT to see what we're talking about.

From cats to mice, let's talk about a certain

fa*mouse* reporter... If you like your funny animals to be a bit more human, like the cast of FUZZY BASEBALL, then you'll love GERONIMO STILTON REPORTER! He's a mouse who is always chasing after a big story for *The Rodent's Gazette*, the number one newspaper in New Mouse City. Perhaps you've even seen his animated adventures on Netflix or Amazon Prime? If so, you'll also enjoy the Papercutz GERONIMO STILTON REPORTER graphic novels.

Then there're the great Nickelodeon characters we publish... SANJAY AND CRAIG features one "funny animal"—Craig, the talking snake—in an otherwise human world. HARVEY BEAKS lives in a world of his own in a mysterious wooded area. BREADWINNERS features SwaySway and Buhdeuce, two talking ducks on the planet Pondgea who deliver bread in their rocket van. PIG GOAT BANANA CRICKET takes place on a world where everything seems to be alive—even bananas! Of course, our biggest hit Nickelodeon title is THE LOUD HOUSE, based on the adventures of Lincoln Loud and his ten sisters—but they have quite a few pets as well: Fangs, a bat; Walt, a bird; Bitey, a mouse; Hops, a frog; Geo, a hamster; Cliff, a cat; and Charles, a dog.

Believe it or not, Papercutz publishes plenty of graphic novels that feature humans, but even as I say that, I notice that the latest THE ONLY LIVING GIRL graphic novel features a story with all sorts of creatures and monsters! I'm not sure if Papercutz is a comics publishing company or a zoo! Hey, what does it matter if they're all great comics?

And speaking of great comics, don't miss another all-new FUZZY BASEBALL story in which the Fernwood Valley Fuzzies travel to Japan to face the Sashimi City Ninjas! Don't miss FUZZY BASEBALL BLAST, available at booksellers everywhere. Check out the next few pages for a special sneak preview!

Thanks,

Jim

STAY IN TOUCH!
EMAIL: salicrup@papercutz.com
WEB: papercutz.com
TWITTER: @papercutzgn
INSTAGRAM: @papercutzgn
FACEBOOK: PAPERCUTZGRAPHICNOVELS
REGULAR MAIL: Papercutz, 160 Broadway, Suite 700, East Wing,
              New York, NY 10038

A MEMO FROM THE COMMISSIONER

John Steven Gurney grew up outside of Philadelphia, Pennsylvania watching helplessly as the Philadelphia Phillies continually lost to the Cincinnati Reds, (and pretty much every other team as well). Then, miraculously, the Phillies won the 1980 World Series, and it seemed as if miracles were possible. John studied Illustration at Pratt Institute in Brooklyn, New York, and was a New York Mets fan in 1986 when the Mets won the World Series. And John was a Boston Red Sox fan in 2004, raising his family in Vermont, when the Red Sox broke free of their 86 year old curse and won the World Series.

As a child John never played organized baseball, only pick-up games in his neighborhood. As an adult he coached tee-ball, was an assistant coach for Small Fry, and was a helpful parent during Little League.

Fuzzy Baseball is John's first graphic novel. John is the author and illustrator of the picture book **Dinosaur Train**, and he is the illustrator of over 140 chapter books, including The **A to Z Mysteries** and **The Bailey School Kids**.

LEARN MORE ABOUT JOHN AT JOHNSTEVENGURNEY.COM.

KIT OCELOT
RELIEF PITCHER

BO "THE GRIZ" GRIZZLY
MANAGER & FIRST BASE

KAZUKI KOALA
RIGHT FIELD

PERCIVALE PENGUINO
BACKUP CATCHER

PEPE PERRITO
SECOND BASE

PAM THE LAMB
LEFT FIELD